Quick! Quick!

Written by Roderick Hunt
Illustrated by Nick Schon,
based on the original characters
created by Roderick Hunt and Alex Brychta

OXFORD
UNIVERSITY PRESS

Read these words

quick	**ou**t
ouch	stu**ck**
sti**ck**	j**a****ck**

4

The ball shot off.

"I can get it," said Kipper.

But Kipper got stuck.

Biff ran to get Dad.

"Kipper is stuck," said Biff.

"I can get him out," said Dad.

"He is still stuck," said Biff.

Dad rang Mum.

"Kipper is stuck," said Dad.

Mum got a big stick.

"Ouch," said Kipper. "I am still stuck."

Wilma ran to get her dad.

"Kipper is stuck," said Wilma.

Wilma's dad got his jack.

This jack will get him out.

Kipper got out.

Dad was stuck.

Talk about the story

A maze

Help Kipper get the ball.